FREE SQUILLY!

FREE SQUILLY!

one squirrelly call to save life

a grown-up child's true freedom fight handbook

ROSAN ARRCYE

TATE PUBLISHING & *Enterprises*

Published by Tate Publishing & Enterprises, LLC
127 E. Trade Center Terrace | Mustang, Oklahoma 73064 USA
1.888.361.9473 | www.tatepublishing.com

Tate Publishing is committed to excellence in the publishing industry. The company reflects the philosophy established by the founders, based on Psalm 68:11,
"The Lord gave the word and great was the company of those who published it."

Book design copyright © 2010 by Tate Publishing, LLC. All rights reserved.
Cover design by Blake Brasor
Interior design by Joey Garrett

Published in the United States of America

ISBN: 978-1-61663-034-8
Fiction / Christian / General
10.03.02

DEDICATIONS

To...

The Holy Trinity—Father, Son, and Holy Spirit—and to God's church. Their leading revealed words, insight, and light in this story.

The Heart of True Americans and their Spirit... In being united, they protect and defend every American right and birthright—thereby, entitling the nation's people, to act and speak freely.

My husband, who changed my life.

His parents, it was Mama's birthday the day this writing was completed.

My family, who are my joy.

My brothers, wholeheartedly, defending life and its real freedom.

My sisters, truly *keeping* life and its many vital secrets.

And to... The Spirit of all God's people devoted to carry out His Flawless Will.

"Their words are like a light shining in a dark place, understand no prophecy in Scripture ever came from the prophets themselves or because they wanted to prophesy. It was the Holy Spirit who moved the prophets to speak from God."

2 Peter 1:19–21

TABLE OF CONTENTS

INTRODUCTION

The author has used a pen name, and identities within the story are changed. In this way, the Spirit communicated without prejudice or favoritism, stemming from someone's status or lack thereof. The main characters in the story, the Ciampis, are born and baptized Catholic. They've always had evident love for God. The pair, called to a new life following Christ, was reborn and water baptized into Christianity after marrying.

Dedicated to spreading the truth of God's Word, the couples' only preference to religion is that everyone should know Christ's true purpose was saving the world! They hope realizing this truth, all peoples will unite in love, achieving Christ's perfect will. Both are deeply thankful; indebted, to family and Christian leaders—Catholic and Protestant—for lighting their path during dark times.

But more importantly, they're *grateful* to the church for sending God's truth, into all nations. Without the active energy of these brave saints, the world is doomed to destroy itself. The author wants each reader to be certain there was no intention to challenge readers to save the world. Total control was given to the Holy Spirit's right to command.

It's key to know the writing took place during High Holy Days—Jewish Passover and Christian Easter. The Holy Spirit initiated, directed, and guided the book throughout this sacred season, when believers around the world thank God for saving them. These faithful ones celebrate the Holy Spirit's perfect promise of eternal life with Him in the Resurrection. The Holy Spirit is always very timely. The book's completion during this extraordinary season makes His principal role even more important and prominent!

The author's prayer is to keep His divine direction … *Every believer devoted to following Christ's perfect plan for saving the world should be rightly rewarded; the Holy Spirit raising them, and their families, into a genuine true life of His Love; giving each His ultimate gift of new life in the Resurrection, today and forever!*

A true incident, the story occurred more than ten years ago. Anyone hearing the tale encouraged the writing, but the perspective from which to tell the story was never made known. Recently, the Holy Spirit provided the order—His point of view to record the narrative. Following His lead, the story is now presented.

The situation takes place in New York State at a residence built in the 1700's. Interestingly, the home was indicated as shelter on George Washington's

Troop Map, during the American Revolution. Truth being stranger than fiction, the house is a perfect setting for the tale. The hero and heroine, Raymond and Rosemarie Ciampi, are veterans of a twenty-year marriage at the time of the story. They're compelled to save a baby squirrel trapped by a cruel fate. This life-and-death situation forces the couple to face their true moral character.

They have a decision... Should they get involved saving the squirrel or ignore the whole situation? The choice makes them question their feelings for each other, and each consideration brings more doubt. If the squirrel dies can they live with that? Or might their indifferent attitude jeopardize the marriage? The Ciampis' heart and future is shaped by the outcome. Difficult confrontations and embarrassing arguments are used by the Holy Spirit. This teaches the couple about justification and standing up for what's right.

Typically, one's well-being and sense of security controls a situation. That makes it much easier to avoid dispute than to face conflict. A person's potential opportunities can be damaged by defending values. Moral principles and ethics come under outside attack; therefore, it takes incredible character to shield those ideals. Backing down and agreeing with hurtful estimations is a much easier course of action. Still, isn't acting uprightly the one sure, decisive answer in every challenge?

Consciously, or sub-consciously, the dilemma faces everyone. Recognizing this test makes a difference in life's outcomes. God is awesome, He's willing to check any action—everything is possible through Christ. Permit Him control and remarkable plans will be achieved. This unique squirrel story, *Free Squilly*, gives true encouragement to the reader. Bank on God's Holy Spirit ... Amazing dreams become reality, when a person's belief is in His Love!

A SQUIRRELLY DILEMMA

I t was early spring, and the clear blue morning sky, still, possessed real warmth. A blush of ripe peach glowed on the horizon. Meanwhile, deep persimmon streaks displayed striking designs, all throughout the pale coral hue. Last evening, the Weather Channel had predicted mild temperatures of sixty degrees. Today would be one of the best so far. Rosemarie could barely remember that kind of forecast—it had been forever. She stepped from bed, looking forward to the day.

Winter drained all enthusiasm by now, so this time of year was really welcome. She couldn't wait to experience that warm sunshine on her skin, the sunny touch that makes a person especially aware it's good to be alive! Rosemarie literally sensed the excitement; it ran through her entire body. She couldn't wait to get outside, after being cooped up indoors the whole winter long.

Wonderfully, the weather person seemed to be right. The day just began, and already it was delightful. Rosemarie started toward the kitchen. The spring mood had her relishing that first cup of coffee. She decided it would taste particularly good outside in the warm air. Soon they'd have breakfast on the outdoor patio. Birds were singing; nothing could possibly be wrong. This was an exceedingly, pleasant day.

Thoughts about the coming summer were Rosemarie's only expectations; the anticipation filled her conscious being. Suddenly logic brought her to awareness, and she became all too alert. There was a loud clamor, of chirping birds. The noise, urged her to open the patio door. Happily smiling, she stepped outside. There was a baby squirrel in the bare primrose bush; but something was wrong. Could her eyes be deceived?

She strained to see … The animal was busy eating seeds; then he'd scurry up and down the oak tree, retrieving more of them. Except, what was that around his neck? It looked like some sort of collar. He was a baby, and it couldn't be affecting him now. Only, how did it get there? She didn't have much time to scrutinize, because the squirrel unexpectedly, ran off about his business, leaving her baffled. What the heck had she actually just witnessed?

Her husband, Raymond, had awakened. He, of course, was mildly puzzled. Why wasn't the aroma of freshly brewed coffee greeting him this morning? He was feeling an energetic, high-spirited anticipation, from this fresh spring day. She rose from bed earlier, to experience that same sensation. Rosemarie proceeded to inform him of this perceived crisis; it was the oddest occurrence concerning a wild baby squirrel.

She believed there was a collar around his neck; the squirrel *must* be someone's pet. Rosemarie was questioning now, "Raymond, don't you think that's probably the situation? Someone must've trained the little guy to turn up at our house. Otherwise, who would put a collar on a baby squirrel? If it wasn't a pet, that would be cruel!" However, the couple didn't want to worry.

Rosemarie even began to deceive herself... What she'd seen wasn't a collar at all; it was merely a shadow. Finally, they placed their thoughts at rest, and started on breakfast. This first meal of the day was what they needed—a buffer to detach from the animal, so any real priorities could be handled. The pair had planned a few spring chores, to make the house feel new again. There's no better feeling than preparing for summer.

This wonderful day gave them every reason to be thankful! It was silly to worry about a wild animal— this was only a squirrel. They shouldn't be so concerned, except Rosemarie's compassionate considerations, were influencing her attention. She deliberated... Could the Ciampis' values be confused? At this moment she believed they were; and the emotion tugged at her heart all through breakfast.

She knew what she'd seen. Right now that little guy was just a baby—he could still eat. Only the squirrel might be wandering loose with no owner; growing larger would definitely cause the collar to greatly, tighten on his neck. Eventually the tiny animal could starve to death. Rosemarie felt no peace with these concerns. She bombarded her husband, with the blurry details in a whirlwind, of horrific conclusions.

Some of this responsibility and guilt just had to dissipate. She wanted to enjoy the day they planned. It's funny. People think placing their insecurity on a loved one improves any situation. What a human deception! Yet being human, a person needs some way to get from beginning to end. On the other hand, if it's only a way of tricking themselves, is that really a good tactic?

Anyway, Raymond wanted to enjoy this day as well. It was their first invitation to be active after the winter's captivity. Rosemarie needed to believe everything was all right; so Raymond hoped to confirm her trust. He proceeded, "Would anyone put a collar on a wild animal, unless it was their pet? Both of us are ridiculous thinking about this." He was reasoning the entire situation to her with absolute confidence!

In order to calm her fears, he continued, "Probably a nest was in someone's tree; then over the course of the winter, branches had fallen. The tree needed pruning and gardeners must've discovered the nest, while cutting back the trees. That scared off the mother... The baby squirrel had been abandoned. Possibly, a concerned homeowner even used the collar to make him a pet—it was that simple!" Her husband did make sense. The whole situation, really, wasn't that complicated.

Sure! People fed birds and squirrels in their neighborhood all the time. Rosemarie was convinced the little guy must have a safe home. This squirrel *definitely* ate fresh nuts and roamed freely, having no restrictions ever. Finally she calmed down. There was just no reason for alarm. Nevertheless, thoughts about that awful collar kept troubling her ... *if that strap wasn't a restriction, what was?*

They finished breakfast and cheerfully prepared for the day ahead. Luckily, each had some precious free time to use sprucing up the yard; so dressed and enthusiastic, they headed outside. Immediately, Raymond was able to see the squirrel, on the oak tree branch. This furry little ball of grey looked happy enough munching on his little finds; yet something was definitely wrong. Clearly some type of band, was wrapped around the animal's neck.

Neither of the Ciampis wished to express their convictions. However, both knew that continued growth would cause a slow, painful death. The tightening collar would prevent proper food intake causing starvation. Even so, their mind became filled with these misgivings: the squirrel was a wild animal, they could be bitten, he might even be rabid! No doubt he might starve to death; still, there wasn't anything that could be done.

NOT MY PROBLEM!

I n any case, the couple made up their mind the squirrel belonged to someone else. That person *certainly* put the collar on him; otherwise, who in their right mind would do this? Why would someone intentionally hurt a baby animal? Nonetheless, one thing couldn't be debated—the squirrel didn't put the collar around his own neck! The Ciampis searched for a hundred explanations, longing to overlook the whole predicament, by ignoring what they saw.

Obviously it was a refusal to face facts. They considered trappers and wildlife agencies, hoping for an easy way out. They believed these experts would solve the dilemma. Only, first they had to consider the cost. Would an expert charge for this type of service? Perhaps, an endangered animal is criterion; then a government agency can provide free help, in a community. At any rate, it's always easy to concede in these types, of testing situations.

Individuals will trust another person's qualifications with no trouble. It's easy for human nature ... They'll determine anybody's experience, to cope with problems. Rosemarie and Raymond were no different. Giving all concerns to a more knowledgeable authority removed the Ciampis' responsibility. They could feel relieved about the squirrel, and concentrating on their assignments would be possible.

Why should they bother themselves with this? It was so easy! A wildlife agency was the answer—this was none of their business. They observed the young squirrel going about his busy activities for the day. His playful romping through the trees made him appear very free indeed! However, watching the Ciampis get ready for their clean-up must've worried the animal; because he suddenly disappeared, into the woodsy area at the side of the yard.

Raymond continued with his yard work. He raked the winter's debris, filling large bags with broken twigs, dead branches, and leaves. Rosemarie washed all the outdoor furniture, then afterward she cleared, and swept the patio. The pleasing lawn was perfection. Dreaming was easy ... The couple pictured relaxing on a hot summer day. They were resting under a tree feeling soft, gentle breezes. A steamy sun, too warm for comfort made the cooling shade, gladly accepted.

Even more than that, those shady spaces and light summer winds were *eagerly* longed for. The couple formed fanciful imagery ... They were enjoying tall, icy glasses of lemonade, along with a plate of cookies. They could almost feel their hammock gently swaying in the breeze. Genuinely that's heaven on earth! The Ciampis couldn't wait—it was a wonderful feeling. The jobs they set out to do were finished, and the place looked great.

Also gratefully, the little squirrel had vanished ... Their problem was gone. Of course, everyone knows that out of sight, means out of mind. The couple decided there had never been anything to worry about. See, everything in their world was right. Nevertheless, Rosemarie felt this little twinge of guilt. She brushed the emotion aside, refusing to be distressed. Both of them were too tired to worry.

Thankfully, their day was over. Lunch had consisted only of a small piece of crumb cake. Hastily, it was washed down with a mug of coffee; then it was back to work. Each had been preoccupied with obtaining results. So now, their attention became concentrated on dinner. It was unbelievable ... They never realized, just how hungry this whole day's work had made them.

ABOUT THE HOUSE

Rosemarie started organizing the kitchen for dinner. She loved to cook. There was always something homemade gracing the kitchen—freshly baked bread, pies, cakes, even homemade macaroni. This always added to the genuineness of the early century home; their life here was blessed. The house had been built with expert skill in the early 1700's. It suited the Ciampis perfectly.

A carpenter by trade; Raymond restored all the original moldings in the house, and refinished the authentic white pine wood, throughout. The couple even fashioned new fish scale shingles, to replace deteriorated wood, on the face of the home. Then, for adding extra shelf space; Raymond *cleverly* created a new built-in pine china closet, for holding dishes and the like. The cabinet was characteristic of all appropriate style and workmanship, to complement the early century construction perfectly.

Their china design had the most delicate, tiny primrose pattern detailed, with twenty-four-karat gold. The graceful set, crafted in the 1800's, was ideally matched to the home's sincerity, and architecture. The set belonged to Rosemarie's grandparents. Her grandmother used it when she was a bride. Their well-designed dining set was equally pleasing to the eye. Manufactured in the 1900's, it had been created with elegant, inlaid flowers.

Quiet green leaves, and pink petals, enhanced the chairs and the breakfront. Choosing a more tasteful set for this particular home would've been impossible. Rosemarie's parents were thrilled to find the dining set. They had just married. The dignified set was already an antique then. Considered in excellent condition, the set was beautiful. Her parents treasured it; and Rosemarie and Raymond cherished this special set, as well.

The Ciampis' home was a true picture of old world charm; yet it was richly flavored with modern warmth, and hospitality. Family and friends loved to come for dinner, or even just to get together. The ambience in the house was infectious; sensing the warmth of living in an earlier day was really possible. Perhaps, it's all this naturalness that makes the story so appealing. A harmony with nature, during that earlier century was actually, easy to understand.

Lifestyles were simpler then; things were slower. Today, cell phones are endlessly ringing, society is overly absorbed: technology, materialism, work. People barely notice their own children's needs. How could they have time to worry about a wild animal? That's why; the Ciampis could never imagine a little squirrel would rock their world! Who would dream an animal could have a part, in shaping the character, and destiny of someone's future?

Looking back, Rosemarie could never be more thankful. These were real life lessons they learned. Important teachings about trusting the Spirit's guidance; even when fear clearly shouts "Walk away, walk away!" No one realizes this dependence is the key that determines the condition of their existence. God gave each the free will to choose. He can't and won't take that away—a freedom of choice.

The Holy Spirit can only influence actions. He isn't allowed to make choices for a person. It's one's own free will that controls the outcomes in life. It takes great courage to let fear go and be used by the Spirit. The Holy Spirit needs permission to guide and establish the end result. If allowed, *"He'll work good things for those who love God"* (Romans 8:28).

Rosemarie placed important significance on the Spirit's values. Faith in God, family loyalty, decency—these standards were the most important aspects of living. All this remained in thought as she prepared the supper. Obviously, it was no surprise that mental images of the little squirrel, being choked by a mistaken collar, *persistently* showed up in Rosemarie's mind.

A VIRTUOUS FAMILY

Setting the lovely primrose dishes on the table, Rosemarie heard her grandmother's accountability. It was a scolding, reprimanding, upright manner... "How can Rosemarie make believe everything's all right. She's been raised with enough values. Animals are under man's authority to be *properly* used for man's benefit. God's creatures aren't to be abused by some immoral individual!"

Her grandmother believed the apple never fell far from the tree. And that virtuous tone confirmed an inherited wisdom, in her granddaughter's heart. Again Rosemarie felt a pulling at her chest—there was no way to ignore the feeling. Breathing deeply, she tried to concentrate on the meal. Supper was ready... So changing her focus, Rosemarie called Raymond to the table. He'd been watching the evening news.

After work, and showering, the NBC Nightly News was a ritual. It kept Raymond's mind all too busy. He formed thoughts on world affairs—focusing on the economy, cost of living increases, housing prices, mortgage rates. This seemed reason enough to develop indigestion at anytime; but right before dinnertime, it appeared inevitable. Yet the news teams are quite an influence with their estimations and opinions.

They manipulate one's attention into captivity at the worst possible moments. Keeping that perspective in mind, it seems astounding—how are Americans considered one of the most overweight peoples anywhere? The nation should be emaciated, from taking on the world's problems. Obviously, the stress has the opposite effect on most persons. Anyway, like many others, Rosemarie was in constant battle with the extra pounds.

An Italian wife that loves to cook finds this a hugely difficult struggle. Italian heritage centers around family and good health. The main focus is always on eating well, with important attention directed, to having the family enjoy the food sufficiently. Now translate that, by stating "eat 'til your tummy's so full your belt pops open!" Undeniably, that's a complete understanding of dinnertime, at an Italian table.

Rosemarie recalled, even when she was a young child, her parents always explained this standpoint: "Children need to grow strong. It's vital to finish everything on the plate." They made sure it was understood that "People are starving in the world—food should never be wasted!" Rosemarie and Raymond were identically raised. Therefore, the Ciampi household was very typical. These memories had hunger pangs nudging Rosemarie, urging her to the table with the cooking.

She set out fried chicken, fresh homemade biscuits, and mashed potatoes with gravy. There was even a nice, fresh salad with tomatoes. Rosemarie learned leafy green vegetables and salads were very important. Her mom considered an inventive tossed salad, with oil and vinegar dressing, essential at the finish of a large meal. A wonderfully knowledgeable cook, she remarked continually about acidity in vinegar promoting proper digestion.

The Ciampis were lucky to have strong, good families. Both Rosemarie's grandparents, and parents, purchased homes within one block of their church. Her grandmother walked each day to pray at the altar, for the needs of loved ones. Her mom content to care for family, sang beautiful songs all day; cheerfully encouraging everyone, by a kindly spirit. These were great woman of faith.

They taught Rosemarie the importance of fearing God's jealous reproof; and gave her trust to believe in God's perfect love. Raymond's parents had great passion for God, as well. They helped build the new Italian church in their neighborhood; and the family held Bible study in their home, twice every week. Rosemarie reflected on the meaning of family—the Ciampis could be rightfully, proud of their upbringing.

Now with the food presented on the table, the couple took their seats. Both were starved, and everything smelled great! Except, *oh no!* Why had she set her mind on the word starved? Rosemarie recognized the familiar heaviness within her heart; and instantly every thought became caught up with the little squirrel. It seemed impossible to enjoy dinner. How could they? That helpless baby animal would be confronted with starving to death—perhaps very soon!

VOICING CONCERNS

How could they ever overlook this incident? Did either of them possess any real moral fiber? Painstakingly, Rosemarie examined the situation ... *Can a future be possible if a generation closes their eyes to difficult confrontations?* Persons would have to be indifferent, unfeeling, heartlessly cold. It just didn't seem conceivable—the approaching outlook appeared bleak. Rosemarie decided, at least Raymond should enjoy the dinner, even if she couldn't.

Every concern and way of thinking was kept inside her anxious mind; only the horrific emotions were too well-founded. The apprehensions gave clear insight into the couple's personality and character. Worse still, understanding the suspicions gave her a distinct awareness about their marriage. She concluded decisions concerning the squirrel would affect them, maybe forever. Right choices had to be made for everyone's sake.

Concentrating on the little animal now had her total attention. Stubbornly, the distressing sentiments held her captive—who could be this cruel, to endanger a baby squirrel, by choking his neck with that collar? Even a pet trainer couldn't be sure a wild animal would find it's way back to them; especially, if freed too early. The person had to realize the squirrel might starve, or even strangle to death.

None of this made sense. Could someone possibly be that naïve? She decided these opinions were unimportant. What did matter: the squirrel would die, unless he was someone's pet. There must be something that could be done. She tried to focus on eating the meal. Her concerns *must* be voiced; but she'd wait until after dinner. Rosemarie was certain Raymond would understand her worrying.

Of course there would be no problem, if the squirrel was someone's pet; they could surely remove the collar without hindering the animal. He'd find his way home anyway. But if the squirrel wasn't a pet, that was very different. Suppose, he somehow freed himself, by chewing on the leash, until it separated from the collar. Even worse, maybe a trapper or homeowner released him, after taking him from the nest.

Circumstances of this nature were an obvious confirmation that the collar *must* be removed. Or, plainly they'd be allowing the squirrel to die a horrible death! How could they ever live with themselves? They had to try something, anything! The couple definitely needed to figure out a way to help, but how? Their thoughts again went to contacting an agency—a wildlife pre-serve, or perhaps an animal rescue.

Rosemarie looked up several phone numbers. Much to the couple's dismay, there would be no help from any of them. It seems the squirrel had to be trapped; either within the house, in the attic, a basement, or wher-ever—even outside on property grounds, provided it was snared in a cage. Otherwise, the agencies couldn't be of assistance. Rosemarie and Raymond needed a way to catch the squirrel, for help to be available.

Once the animal was captured, a wildlife team could come to remove the collar and set the squirrel free. Other than this situation, how would the agency plan for the squirrel to be around? It was impossible to know... they might waste a whole day, if the ani-mal never showed up. The agent insisted Rosemarie shouldn't be too concerned. He explained that it was unnecessary to worry about the way things look—wild animals are very adaptable.

Encouraging the Ciampis, the representative wished them good luck with the matter. He promised to give any phone support needed; but this was all the agency could offer. Sure, it was easy for them to say "Don't worry too much!" They weren't confronted with seeing the squirrel every day. An agent wouldn't be here, to ignore a tightening collar on the growing animal; or to pretend the problem didn't exist, no matter how the squirrel looked. Rosemarie didn't know how anyone could possibly ignore all this.

However, she was very sure; they could *never* live that way. This meant the task was theirs. She knew it was important to help—in fact, they had to help. Just the same, every fear became incredibly real. What if the squirrel bit them? Then, tetanus shots might be required. Rosemarie heard those needles were very painful! And, how about the cost? Those treatments were said to be incredibly expensive. Really, they might not be able to afford this! Imagine ending up in the poor house to save a squirrel.

HELP NEEDED!

One thing was certain, nothing should die a horrible death like that. There was no turning back. The two of them discussed options. Each recognized, living with their conscience would be impossible; so both agreed to an attempt, at removing the collar. That helpless baby squirrel now became their real mission. The Ciampis thanked God. It was His Holy Spirit, that allowed them this special chance, to be used by Him.

The couple asked for God's intelligence, to know what should be done. True to His Word, God is completely ready to supply each person, with an abundant amount of good sense—His Wisdom. All we have to do is ask. *"For the Lord gives His wisdom, from His mouth come knowledge and understanding"* (Proverbs 2:6).

The Holy Spirit began providing ideas. Raymond

purchased fresh peanuts from the grocery store. He planned to scatter them on the low, natural stone, patio wall. Flat, slate tiles were set evenly, across the whole top; and the wall was directly, in front of that tangle, of branches—the large primrose bush, where they first saw the baby squirrel. Everyday, the nuts were arranged *conspicuously* in hopes of the squirrel discovering them.

Of course, peanuts were very appealing. So naturally, the baby animal enjoyed finding them—he'd eat them happily! The Ciampis watched each day from the kitchen door, asking this prayer... *Let the squirrel keep coming.* Thankfully, he did. The kitchen door was about fifteen feet from the stone wall. A large, slate square formed a step; it had been set, right in front of the door. This low, wide, raised surface made a very comfortable sitting place.

The Ciampis would relax on that step, to wait for their squirrel. In the beginning, the animal was on the primrose bush watching, and inspecting the couple. Then, moving from the bush to the wall; the furry character seemed to carefully study the pair, and wonder... are these two a threat? Obviously, the squirrel still had doubts about the bold intent, of these strange onlookers.

June was well under way, and summer could readily be experienced in the air. The primrose bush was full of small, tender green leaves displaying welcome color. Already, the young buds were ready to burst with a beautiful, sweet smell. Rosemarie and Raymond could imagine their delightful fragrance—that delicate scent gently floating *effortlessly* all through the air. The calming reflection filled their spirits.

It was pleasant waiting outside during these warmer

days. There became a gladness in the anticipation of the fuzzy friend. The Ciampis enjoyed being available; they looked forward to their nature buddy's arrival. He'd grown quite large, and progressively, the collar was much tighter. Yet, he seemed to be less skittish around the two of them. Undoubtedly, the little guy was more aware there wasn't any danger.

Maybe, the young squirrel began to appreciate the Ciampis' presence. The truth was, Raymond never came outside without some peanuts. Rightfully the little fellow began to covet, and protect the treats ever so closely. The Ciampis would display the nuts in a delightful feast—the squirrel's very own celebratory delight. Soon their indulgent friend would show up, and wholeheartedly devour that meal.

Rosemarie and Raymond were in attendance to keep him company. The squirrelly little rascal enjoyed their nearness, just as much as feasting! So day by day this continued; the collar became tighter on the growing squirrel; and Rosemarie grew more anxious viewing the conditions. Meanwhile, the same tugging had her worrying … How long would it be before the collar caused real discomfort to the squirrel? Perhaps it was hurting him even now. She could only hope they hadn't fed him too many nuts; unknowingly fattening him up for the kill.

TIME TO ACT

Rosemarie began questioning the condition of their actions... Were they helping the squirrel live, or speeding up his death? Just, what exactly were they doing? Although at this point, a strong feeling of insecurity held her in check anyway. She could "see" herself reaching out to help the small animal. His head was turned, with that neck bowed very low—suddenly her whole body shivered, from an actual feeling of pain.

There was the sensation, of sharp razor teeth sinking into her skin—the "small needle daggers" piercing *whatever* the squirrel supposed might cause him harm. She could feel the stinging. No wonder time was passing, and the Ciampis weren't completing the task at hand. The problem was their fear. Only this caution and hesitancy was endangering the very existence they set out to save—the squirrel's life.

Otherwise, why had they bothered to lure the animal, all this while? The couple agreed … It would be now or never. Raymond began placing nuts, in a trail, leading to the step. At first, the squirrel was skeptical. Soon enough, his desire for the nuts won out. He came closer and closer. The Ciampis would stay very still; and before long that squirrel began taking nuts, directly from Raymond's hand.

Rosemarie was undeniably nervous; but she abandoned the anxiety, in favor of improving the situation. She wished only to rescue the little squirrel's existence. It was this intention that made her think these words: Oh ye, of little faith! If only you will believe, I will show you great things of which you know not. *"Call to me, I will tell you great things beyond your reach of knowledge"* (Jeremiah 33:3).

The Ciampis' upbringing, taught them to be very grounded in God's Word. There could be no doubt about their seat of thought in the experience. They knew this would be impossible for them without the Spirit's guidance. It was easy to see the two were called to act in the affair … And, the couple understood their choice backward and forward. If they determined other than to be used by God; both would regret that decision for a very long time.

Believing and trusting God to complete the task became their strength. They discovered meaning in the circumstance, and learned value from what was taking place. It wasn't about this one action of removing a collar from a little squirrel; this sole, particular state of affairs with a wild animal. The outcome in this incident, would cause them to rethink all their selections in everything.

They were being instructed by the Holy Spirit. The couple was making deliberate decisions—believing, trusting, choosing to give the Spirit control; this was a heartfelt way of life. It appears trouble-free; nonetheless it's more filled with problems, than anyone would imagine. Still, a just God gives great rewards for completing His will. This said, the Ciampis could thoroughly agree the squirrel was no one's pet. Even in all this time, the collar was never removed.

The band was noticeably tighter on the animal's neck. This made the couple understand it was time to complete the task—tomorrow would be the day. Prayers focused, they went to sleep. The following morning both were ready. Each was peaceful, prepared, and their thoughts were fixed. They hoped this little dependent would show up soon. In their usual manner, the pair rested comfortably on the outside step.

Sure enough, the squirrel arrived for his nuts. He came very close, wanting to retrieve his rewards from Raymond's hand. Rosemarie reached out, managing to catch hold of the furry frame. Capturing the squirrel unaware, she grasped the main part of his body firmly. That same moment, Raymond caught hold of the animal. Using his free hand, he created a second, more reliable support. The small hairy form was doubly trapped. They had the little guy!

Her husband was in complete control, holding the squirrel securely, with both hands. Rosemarie quickly ran inside, while trying to make the correct decision. Which would cut the collar loose without any problems—large scissors, or a sharp knife? She needed the fastest, best method. Not being sure, she opted for both. They hadn't planned this earlier, because it was necessary to know about the material. What was the collar made from?

The substance was of very strong twisted nylon threads. They weaved together tightly, to form an exceptionally durable, flat type of rope. It was secured with a buckle on one end, and fastener holes on the other. The little squirrel seemed confused; his small body shivered with fright. Yet he wasn't squirming, or even trying to escape. Much to their amazement, the squirrel didn't even attempt to bite. In fact, he wasn't attacking either of them in any way.

The animal must've sensed they were trying to help. Thankfully, all Rosemarie's fears and anxieties had been for nothing. Being able to recognize it would go this perfectly; there was no need to panic at all. Of course, Rosemarie should've known—when God calls, He brings His people through. She knew about the promises from reading the Bible. Only they were just words on paper.

It's necessary to apply belief and trust for a person's faith to grow. That's what increases capability; thereby awarding the believer, with courage and determination to carry out remarkable actions. By giving every care to God and trusting Him, He'll be sure any good plan succeeds. *"Entrust your works to the lord and your plans will succeed"* (Proverbs 16:3).

FINALLY FREE!

At last, it was time to remove the collar. Rosemarie's heart went out to the little squirrel. She detected it was important to keep focused. If she allowed herself to get emotional, she'd never be of any help. Taking a deep breath, she calmed and steadied her hands. Meanwhile, Raymond held the small quivering form, firmly and gently. He already decided, Rosemarie might be terrified using the knife if the squirrel squirmed. His judgment was correct. The whole time, while planning the strategy to achieve the task, she worried ... *what if the knife twists?*

She knew the little animal might be injured—worse, it would be her fault! With as much courage as possible, she made a choice. Taking the scissors, she carefully slid the sharp, open blade under the collar, against the squirrel's neck. That bushy-tailed hoarder seemed almost calm, submissive to his fate. He barely wriggled, and very nearly stopped every movement. The little character must've realized it was important to be still.

The scissor sawed back and forth, again and again. There was nothing; the blades scarcely frayed the edge. Rosemarie used all her strength, but that nylon cord wouldn't budge. True to Murphy's Law, "Anything that can go wrong…" Well, enough of that. It was necessary to cut the cord without any delays; the Ciampis knew it was crucial. Needless to say, the more anxious Rosemarie became, the longer the job took.

Her heart filled with worry. Imagine if they can't remove the collar after all this! Refusing to entertain these thoughts, she relinquished her position over to her husband. Rosemarie placed her hands on top of Raymond's. At the same time, he allowed his hands to slide away from the submissive, furry frame. She held the small, compliant squirrel securely; then maneuvered the animal, gently into position.

Competently, she removed him from Raymond's lap, to place him on her own. She could scarcely believe it. That fuzzy little rodent wasn't being aggressive, or trying to break away from them at all! Raymond took hold of the scissor now. Again, the precise open blade was slid under that choking neckband, flat against the squirrel's neck. The squirrel complied, staying quiet and motionless.

Raymond forced down on the two blades with a determined physical power. He pressed the cutting edges together tightly. In one strong, quick slash; the collar broke loose. Suddenly popping off and up; the band lurched high into the air. This prized valuable, so difficult to recover; finally came to rest on the slate, patio floor. Rosemarie reached out, and gathered the collar into her hands. Quietly, she stared at the thin strap that held the baby animal prisoner.

Each of them could see the faded color, the filth that distorted the once brightly, dyed green cords. The rusted buckle was a testimony confirming their method—there would've been no other way to remove that collar. Immediately, the squirrel looked up at them; he was calm and thankful to be free! Decisively, Rosemarie and Raymond released the young animal. The squirrel seemed stunned. Yet surprisingly, he leaped from the couple's lap, and their presence.

Determinedly, he ran onward, toward the familiar primrose bush. There, he camouflaged himself inside the bushes, dense growth. The Ciampis, again, observed the squirrel's appearance. He made his way up, onto the branches of the oak tree. Then abruptly stopping; the young animal looked back, as if in complete gratitude. Gradually, he turned away and scurried off; leaving them behind.

Moving *persistently* far and high, in through the trees; at last the precious, wild friend disappeared from sight. The Ciampis stared in disbelief, while holding that faded green collar. Never were they more certain of anything—no material item could feel as significant. Saving that little squirrel's life was unbelievable. More than that, it was remarkably humbling. There was a lot to be thankful about. If it had gone any other way … Well, the Ciampis just refused to be burdened with those thoughts.

They had trusted the Holy Spirit, and believed Him for guidance. There could be no doubt that God used them. Rosemarie and Raymond could take pleasure in this satisfaction, rightfully. Their many cares about making worthy choices were quiet and calm. It was clear—by choosing correctly, life was saved. *"Today, I set before you life and death. Choose life, that you and your descendents may live"* (Deuteronomy 30:19).

The Spirit had confirmed their interpretation; it was His leading they heard! These insights hadn't occurred to the Ciampis, when first facing this predicament. They could only wonder why the decision should be so significant. Ultimately, they understood. The choice about the squirrel's existence would affect their relationship, for a very long time.

Choosing life never looks difficult. Nevertheless, it's exceptionally hard to do, because the size of the pathway is limited. The Spirit hoped to enlighten them further. Their minds were open, and a brightness came through this Scripture: *"The path to real life is narrow. And few are those who find it"* (Matthew 7:14).

The meaning in that Verse became a clear groundwork. The choice for life involves impossible confrontations. Repeatedly, obstacles are thrown across the way, making it appear much more sensible to rethink every choice. Choosing life lays a foundation for the future; it affects everything and everyone around. Relationships with family, friends, even business dealings will be influenced. Not everyone will be comfortable with the new direction.

Everything will be different, and they won't understand. These are confrontations none of us want to deal with. Rosemarie and Raymond only knew this was the choice they made. It felt wonderful. Both of them wanted to stay on this course forever. They were amazed by the whole episode; the little wild squirrel never even attempted to bite them. The young animal stayed in their grasp, with incredibly little resistance, allowing them to remove that collar.

This comprehension that the squirrel's life was saved became one of the most awesome experiences imaginable. And accepting that amazing feeling, the Ciampis needed time to consider—the noble sense of gratification would *certainly* be an important element of reward. Balance would be key; especially in certain careers—for instance firefighting, or law enforcement.

Rosemarie and Raymond suspected that working in fields of this type; emotions would be heightened. Easily, pride could destroy those skilled capabilities, turning the workman useless. Competency of this kind should never be taken for granted. The Ciampis were developing sensitivity, a genuine passion for these life-saving circumstances. For the first time, since being affected by the issue; each became *incredibly* conscious of life. Neither could conceive of a more valuable commission, than the appointment to save lives.

An invitation, or call, to save living beings is truly a special contribution—a real talent. Raymond and Rosemarie were incredibly thankful for their small, though minor, share in the opportunity. They never supposed more good could be in store up ahead … Or that the noteworthy benefits would develop moral fiber and character, giving them a much greater quality of existence. In any case, since encountering the squirrel, neither felt any motivation to name the rascal. Yet, that furry creature had become quite a part, of their every-day living.

A NAME OF DISTINCTION

Understandably; designating a name emerged trivial in comparison to the condition, of the squirrel. The events that were happening made a happy, pet name seem inappropriate—even wrong. Caring if the squirrel lived or died was the only concern; so distressing over a name would've been ridiculous. However with the animal safe, it seemed like the right time. Rosemarie and Raymond, both, came up with ideas. Interestingly, the name *Squilly* popped to mind. *Squilly the Squirrel* … That was catchy.

For some reason, *Free Willy*, that friendship story about a young boy and a killer whale had their thoughts. Of course! *Willy, Squilly*—no wonder the name flowed so easily! Anyway, that whale touched every heart. In the story, greed exhibits an ugly face, weaving it's web of destruction and near death. Only love can correct the confusion. Yet a happy ending of equal consideration, persuaded the couple to ponder "their" squirrelly narrative ... *Free Squilly!*

Neither, would figure out *why* the collar was on *Squilly's* neck. But the pair was secure knowing their wild friend was no longer restricted and unable to eat. At last, he was able to enjoy his normal, untamed existence. Many people formed opinions; and each questioned factors, and influences affecting the environment, around the home. Although no one could figure, what actually caused the issue to take place.

However; the meaningful future happenings, or occurrences would be impossible to invent, or dream up. More remarkable was this fact ... Choices concerning a little squirrel made such substantial, inner importance about life become unveiled. Now several hours had passed since *Squilly* was liberated. The Ciampis began to wonder where he'd gone. The squirrel was always somewhere close by. Yet oddly, he was nowhere to be found.

The pair decided maybe, the stress of removing that choking collar scared *Squilly,* causing him to disappear. They expressed a further doubt—able to act freely, would he just run away, as far from here as possible? The Ciampis considered some actualities ... Could *Squilly* feel a lighter weight difference about his neck? Wearing a ring or gold chain for any length of time; when the article is removed a significant change is felt, on the flesh in that area.

There's a sense of something missing; a lighter weight, where the object is usually worn. It's particularly noticeable. Would a squirrel feel that distinction as well? Later that day, *Squilly* was back. Obviously, the squirrel's hunger had gotten the better of him. Raymond figured the little character overcame any shock experienced, deciding in favor of some fresh nuts. Instinctively, he allowed Raymond to hand feed him.

The Ciampis were overjoyed! *Squilly* was free, and would still come to visit. Their little animal wasn't afraid of them. But the couple could feel especially good, because the creature was out of harm's way—he was no longer in danger. Even more than that, their furry buddy would be a fun neighborhood pet! Nevertheless, the Ciampis had no indication the squirrel was already very attached to them. *Squilly* was becoming their special friend.

AN AMERICAN HERITAGE

The early eighteenth century home was an American Colonial Saltbox. Constructed with low ceilings and important fireplaces of impressive size; dwelling places in that period were built, to keep a better part of the heat indoors. The lower ceilings, and below-average doorway headers, maintained their design to preserve this degree of hotness, close to the ground. This meant, much of the fiery temperature became very accessible.

Through this process, a body could feel affected by the fair amount of heat, and keeping warm was achievable. Interestingly; the standard of workmanship reduced door heights to such an extent, that many homeowners had to duck lower, to avoid a bump on the forehead. Just as a reference, some doors were perhaps only seventy-two inches in height—today's headers are at least eighty inches.

Yet, this strategy assured currents of cold air and drafts would remain at a minimum. Any high temperature and warmth attained, that amount of warmness was stopped from escaping or leaking out. Back then, only one source provided heat—those great and vital fireplaces. No provisions were made for ceilings of prominent height, and grand extraordinary doorways were luxuries. Knowingly, these gracious homes managed better without them.

The outline of the roof over the kitchen was determined, by that customary structural design. The pitch had a deep easy slant toward the patio. This vital, previous standard affected the door height; it was only about six feet high. The door opened onto the square slate step; and Raymond fed the little guy from there. The squirrel would inspect the large step, from a tree or the roof; just hoping for the couple to arrive.

Easily able to leap, from a branch to the roof; the squirrel moved smoothly, to the border of the roofline; in anticipation of his caretakers' appearance. Raymond would make his way onto the step with nuts in hand. The exceptionally low roof edge; permitted *Squilly* to boldly jump onto Raymond's shoulder. Quickly, the little squirrel would maneuver; away from that strong shoulder, to continue onward; down Raymond's firm arm.

There, the squirrel positioned himself, perched proudly on that solid forearm. Patiently, *Squilly* would wait, expecting to retrieve those treasured nuts—a squirrel with manners! Who would believe it? It didn't take long to find out... The little guy was becoming quite in the habit of showing off his antics. No sooner would the Ciampis step outside; when the furry character would immediately, show up to acquaint himself, with their every action.

Resting his body on his hindquarter, he'd sit along with them, at the patio table. Then he'd step onto Raymond's hand, easily as onto an ordinary, tree branch. He was totally undaunted. All could see this little friend enjoyed performing before a live audience. Of course, any spectators were pleased to have a delightful time; everyone benefited by the good experience.

It was remarkable. Guests would visit and *Squilly'd* steal the show. Everyone was speechless! He swirled from the rooftop, to place himself on Raymond's shoulders. Then, proceeding onto that familiar arm; the squirrel stayed to visit with his audience. The animal was carefree, unconcerned, even with people around—why wasn't he afraid? It seemed impossible. Nevertheless, the exciting entertainment was enjoyed wholeheartedly; it was pure fun!

As summer continued, the Ciampis decided a weekend getaway was in order. Already, the weather was too warm for comfort; so efforts exerted at work seemed boring and repetitive. The financial system had definitely been more acceptable. Really, it was no longer easy to understand what was happening. Reduced expenditures by business were causing a market reduction in sales. These cost-cutting measures and cutbacks intimidated buyers.

Fearful of losing jobs, consumers were reluctant to spend their money. Rosemarie and Raymond felt fortunate... They still had the option of taking a few days leave from work. Families were beginning to feel real pressure. All this strain related to the many, costs of living increases. And it was a fact home prices were rising; making the purchase of a new home, even more difficult.

Everyone was trying to hold onto their paychecks. Whatever the causes, the Ciampis needed a break, from these uneasy circumstances. Now, for the first time since *Squilly* was set free, the Ciampis faced a challenge—*Squilly's* safety. They were being forced to know and understand that domesticating the squirrel, might've endangered him. Bearing that in mind, the couple began to feel accountable, for the squirrel's welfare.

All the joy of befriending the pet was marked, accompanied by a considerable cost. That penalty of price was their responsibility toward the squirrel. There would be no problem, while Rosemarie and Raymond stayed in the house. However if they were to leave, could *Squilly* survive? The squirrel was enormously accustomed to their being around; his usual routine was waiting for the Ciampis to dole out nourishment.

Maybe the squirrel would get confused about searching for his own food. Even more frightening: Venturing into a nearby yard to look for attention, he could find a *nature hater*—a person that dislikes wild animals, believing they only make a mess of the land, around the house. This person might harm or even injure him! *Squilly* was so used to them, so trusting. Rosemarie felt true guilt. How could they have been so selfish?

Sure, it was fun to show *Squilly* off to their friends— he was cool to have around. But, they never considered how dependent he was, or thought about his survival.

What if they needed to leave for some reason, or had to change their residence? Only one action could correct this chaotic state—a reliance on the Spirit, to demonstrate *Squilly* would be here, when they returned. Their heart was in the right place. God would have to respect their plea.

Nevertheless, Rosemarie felt *ridiculously* foolish. Here, she was praising herself and commending Raymond; thinking they were great to save the little animal. Only the entire time, she never figured out that keeping him as a pet was no better, than putting another collar around his neck! They had so much to learn regarding real, heartfelt life. Still, the Ciampis knew it was time to get away; they needed a breather from laboring at that job. Their trust just couldn't be in themselves. And *Squilly*... he needed to be put back into the right place; where he belonged—in the hands of the Spirit.

As best they could, they presented these caring feelings and reservations, over to a supreme nurturing control. The Ciampis willingly identified with the actuality, that God used them to save *Squilly*. Now, they must earnestly pray *Squilly* would be safe and sound; out of harm's way and secure—under heaven's guardianship. They packed their things, loaded the car, and left for the weekend. *Squilly's* inquiring eyes watched from the rooftop the whole time. It's for sure that squirrel was wondering... where's everybody going?

TRUSTING A GREATER POWER

The Ciampis tried to enjoy their time away. There was only one problem—each understood their childish immaturity. The pair had voiced every thought to each other. That meant, they were able to interpret God's great compassion, toward their irresponsibility. It was way too easy feeling incredibly small. Yet, they were acquiring such new knowledge and wisdom. Who could ever dream a little squirrel would affect their life in so many ways?

Although the couple needed to get away; still they couldn't wait, to return. They hoped their faith and prayers had ensured the squirrel's safety. Nonetheless they were afraid... *what if?* Suppose the little squirrel wasn't there, when they got back. Finally the car pulled into the driveway. Much to their relief, *Squilly* was perched on the front porch table, peeking inside the kitchen window.

This was his usual custom of checking on his care-givers, when they weren't outside. He'd sit on the table, looking into the windowpane to see ... were Rosemarie and Raymond moving about? Then he'd scratch gently at the glass, or the frame around the window, hoping to get their attention. It was curious; he never left any damaging marks. And believe it or not—gaining atten-tion in this manner was an endearing characteristic!

Squilly's playfulness always made them smile. Visibly, the little animal had now spotted their car. Suddenly he bolted onto the rooftop; obviously excited, they were home. The Ciampis felt relieved. They were happy *Squilly* was fine! However, the little squirrel was taught an important lesson—the episode trained him. Rosemarie and Raymond wouldn't understand about the instruction, not for quite a while yet.

The couple dropped every belonging inside the door, and hurried to get *Squilly* his peanuts. Their little friend had waited far too long! Raymond grabbed the jar of nuts, from the cupboard. Hastily, the pair accompanied each other out the door. At once, the squirrel leaped from the edge of the roof, onto Raymond's shoulders. Going non-stop along the familiar arm, the animal positioned himself; comfortably resting on Raymond's forearm, to look at them.

Obviously, the pet wanted them to understand; he was pleased at their return. The Ciampis could feel that liberating freedom from anxiety. Both were glad to dis-cover *Squilly* remembered them, and equally grateful to know the squirrel was well. Their whole weekend conversation was dominated by the little creature's wellbeing. They were like doting parents engaged in scrutinizing the children's distressful behavior.

The longer they expressed opinions, the more their speech exposed every episode, revealing credit and any discredit. Unrelentingly; the couple repeated the issues, mulling over their selfish behavior to reflect performance, and actions. How were they so oblivious to the responsibility, that both only saw the squirrel, as just a fun game? What overconfidence to think they were wonderful—believing *their* caring had saved *Squilly* from starvation.

Rosemarie chided on, "Sure we're terrific—we saved him to abandon him … Now he's worse off than before!" They carried enormous blame over that wild animal; it's truly beyond belief. The couple became very sensitive to their mistakes. Accordingly; spiritual insight about animal activists and agencies like Greenpeace, routed Rosemarie's opinions. Still, she was never the type who believed owning a fur coat was an abomination. Wild animals were under man's dominion, not to be abused; but for the good and enjoyment, of human beings.

However, what about the accountability? Having lesser creatures ranked under human authority was beginning to take root. Rosemarie was learning… Survival, quality of life, maintaining these creatures; all this is unquestionably important. They shouldn't be suffering, not while they live, or at the time of their death—especially if it can be prevented. Thankfully, our heavenly Father is true to His Word. "*I am confident that God is well able to guard all that has been entrusted to me until that day*" (2 Timothy 1:12).

God had absolutely, positively guarded *Squilly;* keeping him encouragingly, well! Rosemarie was beginning to believe; yet she still had doubts—things *might've* gone wrong. It was important for her to be sure the Spirit was clearly understood; there had to be no reason to feel accountable. Of course, she knew their irresponsibility was pardonable. So her direction shifted. These new thoughts were more important.

Rosemarie knew most of all she was grateful for the Scriptures filling her spirit. Every now and then, a key verse came to mind...These Sacred Passages would direct the Ciampis' way. Rosemarie hoped she, and Raymond, could interpret these critical meanings properly. This required the couple consider their actions, paying careful attention to conduct. One thing was sure; both knew there was more caught up here than some good deed, toward a wild animal.

They came to the significant realization this wasn't just about removing a collar from a squirrel's neck. Information, insights concerning wildlife preservation and welfare—all this was new to the Ciampis. These facts and knowledge would be useful, necessary in the future. Of course, they had no idea about this yet. However, Raymond and Rosemarie were obtaining real wisdom, a change in discernment permitting them, to live God's better plan. This was real preparation to assist a hurting world.

The couple found new power, a sincere heartfelt conviction, to know worth in recognizing wrong. And their recently discovered life was represented by changed intelligence. This transformed understanding gave them prudent caution, to figure out the huge burden included, in accepting blame. All these strengths developed a natural gift—the safe, expert skill for appreciating value in accountability.

There was only one obligation: know to let go of reproach; it's as central to aiding others as recognizing wrong. Helping humankind takes resistance, defensive ability, an impressive amount of strength, and courage. Holding onto fault depletes that emotional toughness. Carrying blame, bitterly *insisting* on one's interests— those are self-centered and indulgent. They're more connected to self-pity, than honoring and glorifying God, who created the universe.

People need to be liberated, from the cares of looking after selfish desires. This was a new process of thinking for Rosemarie. She wasn't sure how to agree with these procedures, or follow the methods. Nonetheless, Christians were taught not to blame others. But, let go of *her* feelings of guilt—that might be difficult. *"Judge not lest ye be judged"* (Matthew 7:1; Luke 6:37).

MEANING FROM A CHRISTIAN BACKGROUND

As a young girl, Rosemarie learned instinctively to carry blame, to pick up her cross and follow Christ. Carrying blame was tied to the duty of carrying your cross. How was it possible to release yourself and others of the blame—isn't that selfish? Ignoring the wrong, saying nobody's at fault; that overlooks the pain suffered, by the wronged person. She needed time to make sense of this.

Rosemarie believed blame must be channeled somewhere; or defending right from wrong seemed impossible—when nothing's to blame, wrongs would never be exposed. Then, where's the motivation to do the right thing? Lawlessness and chaos could dominate the world; everyone doing only what's good for them. She found this hard to understand, confusing to accept. It compelled her to think about the *Gospel of Saint John.*

In John Chapter 8: A woman is caught in adultery; she's blamed for her actions by a mob of men. Christ wrote something in the sand, and afterward no one condemned the woman—she was set free. *Could this be the connection decoding how to eliminate blame? Can this be how to identify and acknowledge a wrong?* Rosemarie believed the concepts might be principal in righting a hurtful act. Her mind was settled. She decided that being familiar with the truth of these convictions could be key.

The Ciampis prayed for enlightement, hoping confusion would be changed, into understanding. They tried to open their heart and mind, struggling to be certain of every action. Their desire was to remain in God's service. Reflecting on that Gospel, Rosemarie was filled with inspiration. The Spirit's explanation was explicit: Many people are lost in a dark life without love. Forced into this despondent existence, they reach out for any chance at happiness or peace.

Worrying about hurting someone else would be impossible, because they have too much pain inside. The Spirit urged on, adding extra support for the cause: Christ never blamed the woman for the sin. He didn't allow her to blame herself. Christ commanded her *"Go free. And, sin no more"* (John 8:11). Christ wanted the genuine love she was experiencing to strengthen her; maybe for the first time allowing her to live in happiness—with approval in this arrangement.

Then, a serious concept about forgiveness, answered many questions Rosemarie found confusing. The couple was instructed to release blame; she found this difficult to understand—how would a wrong ever be made right? *Something* had to be accountable for a hurtful action to be pardoned. Otherwise, how could the wronged person feel any peace? All her doubts were justified; then clarified, in this description.

Christ told us to forgive endlessly, if our brother is genuinely sorry. Except He also told us to cut ourselves off from sinners—unrepentant people that are openly not sorry. *"If your brother sins, tell him so, if he repents, forgive him"* (Luke 17:3). Someone honestly sorry is easy to forgive. In true repentance, the person's heart and mind are changed.

"This is the agreement, I will write My laws on their hearts. I will inscribe them on their minds. Their sins I will remember no more. Where there is forgiveness, there is no need for an offering of atonement" (Hebrews 10:16–18). *"If we go on sinning, there is no more atoning for our sin. Vengeance is Mine, says the Lord. It is a fearful thing to be cast into the hands of the Lord"* (Hebrews 10:26–31).

Christ had drawn a line in the sand. It convicted the adulteress woman's accusers, causing them to give up their charge against the woman. God clearly draws a definite line convicting, or acquitting each person. It will be instantly recognizable, where that line is drawn. At last, the Ciampis had real understanding. There's a true distinction between right and wrong. It's God's control that liberates a person's life; His power sets the believer free, to forgive and act in genuine love.

Oddly, that baby squirrel had the Ciampis learning plenty about life. Summer was nearly over, so the couple was already thinking about autumn. *Squilly* was still visiting, and Rosemarie and Raymond were happy to be uplifted by his silly pranks. Then, toward the end of August, the pair began to see less of the squirrel. They speculated, about what was taking place. One day he'd come, but not the next. This went on for a couple of weeks.

Finally early one morning, they awoke to a thumping noise. It seemed to be directly above their bed, but must've come from outside, on the bedroom roof. *Thump. Thump. Thump.* They couldn't figure it out. Half asleep, the pair tried to focus ... *Was an animal getting into the attic?* Rosemarie and Raymond listened intently—everything was still and quiet. Suddenly there it was again. *Thump. Thump. Thump.* It was annoying! Where exactly was the sound pinpointed? And just, what the heck was it?

Even with all the confusion, they weren't ready to leave the sanctity of the bed. It was too comfortable! Only that sound was unrelenting. *Thump. Thump. Thump.* Rosemarie gave in. She propped herself up, to push the covers away. Then, taking a moment to collect herself; she turned and slid her feet down, onto the pine flooring. Feeling the smooth, wide planks; the coolness of that notably, historic white pine wood under her feet; eventually, she became more alert.

Raymond chuckled, relishing in the luxury, of remaining in bed ... *Rosemarie would check on the circumstances.* Lazily she approached the window, needing to see—nothing was there. An enclosed porch was just off the bedroom hallway. Rosemarie continued toward that window. If the problem couldn't be seen from there, she'd have to go outside to look. Now she was praying. The last thing they needed, was a hole chewed in the roof, or any added repair expenses.

Not to mention; even the inkling of a notion that referred to another wild, animal challenge; well that just sent shivers through her entire, essence! Rosemarie directed her eyes out the porch window. Happily, she was able to see—it was *Squilly* on the roof, just over their bed. *Amazing!* Using his paws, to lift the edges of the asphalt roof shingles; he'd repeatedly slap those tiles down, very hard. *Thump. Thump. Thump.*

Just what the heck! Did this crazy squirrel think he was accomplishing something? *Squilly'd* never done anything like this before. This was a novel experience for Rosemarie. So she signaled … Raymond had to look at this; and he'd prefer to see the spectacle, first hand! She couldn't imagine what this process was all about. *Squilly* spotted her at the window, and darted to the roof's edge.

Then, leaping to the apple tree, at the left side of the porch; he disappeared through the branches. She was left totally puzzled. This was a whole new turn of events. Now Raymond was in attendance. Both waited expectantly, keeping lookout at the window. They wondered what the squirrel was doing. The pair began a guessing game … "just why are we witnesses here?" There was no time for thinking up reasons, because apple branches began shifting.

They could see *Squilly's* shape reappear. Swifty, he made his way back from the apple tree, onto the porch roof. Only this time *Squilly* brought a friend—a mate. Together, the two squirrels pranced across the roof, then stopped at the window. *Squilly* moved forward to peek through the glass with eyes that expressed a determined attention. This nature friend was looking toward his two cherished advocates; obviously in search of their approval!

Very meaningfully he'd showed his intelligence, revealing his wishes—it was an unyielding desire. The squirrel wanted both his helpers, Rosemarie and Raymond, focused and involved. The animal was in no rush. Gradually, once secure about this detail; the squirrel "proudly" displayed his new mate, along with their notable relationship.

Perceptively; Rosemarie and Raymond glanced at each other in complete agreement. Then, the couple stared *affectionately* back towards *Squilly*. The Ciampis were smiling favorably, each acknowledging this high-ranking introduction, with pleasure. As if the obligation was now fulfilled, the two squirrels turned from sight, and dashed off the roof. Finally, seemingly satisfied; the furry pair returned themselves, to the apple tree.

LIFE ON A SPECIAL PROPERTY

Obviously, the furry pair began gathering apples. The entire crop wasn't quite completely ripened; but the sugary, tart fruit was more than satisfying; especially for *Squilly* and his little mate. They'd enjoy fresh, crisp, crunchy feasts. Strong, fully extended branches made these fruit trees absolutely beautiful. And in the spring, amazing blossoms flowered—soft, pale, pinkish-white buds; bursting open, to fill the whole neighborhood, with the pleasing fragrance.

The ripened fruit was *incredibly* sweet. Rosemarie and Raymond made many, fresh homemade apple pies, all from those particular apples. Generally neighborhood apple trees tend to bear small tart fruit; it's barely even usable. A large amount gets eaten by birds or wild animals. But these delicious apples were valued, and flavorful. They were every bit as tasty, as high-quality prized fruit—undeniably, equal to crops from the best New York State apple orchards.

As a matter of fact, all the trees gracing the home's property were wonderfully, good looking. Some of the white pines were magnificent, more than two hundred years old. These strong, established trees were easily there, before the house was ever built. Definitely, many pines of similar variety were felled during past times, and used to construct the dwelling. Original clapboard siding, paneling, flooring; all was hewn from this same North American white pine.

There can be no doubt, the fine specimens still standing are vital, elegant signs of an earlier day—a new day when our country was just beginning. Raymond and Rosemarie could imagine the *Squilly* twosome building a very inviting nest, right in one of those grand old trees. But oddly, after that day, they never saw *Squilly* or his little friend again. The Ciampis' weekend disappearance must've communicated a valuable memory to the squirrel.

Plainly, the instruction period was worth remembering. Perhaps, it even presented a key impression about dependency and abandonment. In any case, an accurate lesson had been instilled inside the squirrel's spirit. Evidently, the little animal wanted the Ciampis to appreciate that he was starting a family. The bold prankster figured out he couldn't afford the silly tricks any longer—those mischievous high jinks, which allowed them to enjoy such a good time together.

The environment instructed his training; and by enduring the education, the experience proved useful.

It persuaded *Squilly* that subjecting his family to human intervention would jeopardize them. A combination of difficult circumstances, an actual course of events, made the squirrel know his existence was threatened. Untamed animals deserve to survive in their natural setting. Depending on humans for food can endanger their inborn abilities.

Satisfying needs for themselves, or their families will be full of problems. Likely, living in their natural habitats will cause harm to the animal's welfare. Nature had qualified *Squilly* during the Ciampis' departure, directing the squirrel to guide his family, by inborn instincts. All this was strange to the Ciampis. In spite of that, Rosemarie and Raymond were learning valuable information about nature, wildlife … and *Squilly's* disappearance.

For the most part, individuals view animals as dumb. However, wild animals are part of a Spirit created by God. Human eyes are closed to this power of observation, because natural sight is unable to see the things of the Spirit. The experience gave the Ciampis an advantageous opportunity to be familiar with this all important influence—the Life Force, living within all God's creatures. It was this Spirit that taught *Squilly* to limit his relationship with the Ciampis.

The squirrel ended his connection with the couple, for the sake of his family's safety. *Squilly* loved Rosemarie and Raymond, and became their pet. It couldn't have been easy separating from these benefactors, or those prized peanuts. The squirrel must've learned quite a warning. Rosemarie was now aware—humans needed to care that their actions affect nature. Fully alert, she could see there was meaning in *these* Scriptures:

"All of God's creatures long for the day when there will be no more pain and death" (Romans 8:19–23); *"The earth is full of Your creatures to give them food as they need, You supply, they gather, but if You turn away they panic"* (Ps 104:24–31); *"Happy are those who fear the Lord, who delight in doing His commands, their good deeds will never be forgotten, the righteous will long be remembered"* (Ps:112: 1,3,6); *"Happy are people of integrity, who follow the law of the Lord, walking only in His paths…I will delight in Your principles and not forget Your Word. Open my eyes to see the wonderful truths in Your Laws."* (Psalm 119: 1,16,18)

Their whole experience had been explained in those Passages. It became plain; all creation belongs to God alone. Therefore, learning His principles was the true key, in every life circumstance. The Holy Spirit made it *exceptionally* clear … God keeps and honors the righteous who do His commands. It was unbelievable—how was such insight revealed because of a squirrel's situation? Undeniably, the Holy Spirit can use "anything" to guide those that love and trust God.

The couple now felt a bit astray. Each was missing *Squilly* and his tricks. So by continuing to place peanuts on the wall; Raymond hoped the two squirrels might visit again. For a while, the Ciampis even sat on the step waiting. Yet the furry pair never appeared. Raymond tried leaving nuts outside overnight, thinking that might work. Sure enough, that wall was cleared in the morning. Still, *Squilly* never called on the Ciampis again—at least not known to them.

Eventually, Raymond stopped leaving the nuts. He was unsure, which type of animals were approaching; and neither of the Ciampis wanted rodents remaining, to set up housekeeping. The couple would see squirrels playfully chasing one another, up and down the oak trees, just beyond the patio—although none ever came closer. They'd only rest on branches eating their seeds, or whatever was in season at the time.

Sometimes it seemed they were on lookout, watching Rosemarie and Raymond observing them—like a game! Directing their eyes at the Ciampis, they'd keep very still; just until the two humans made faces, of some sort. Then, the squirrels would react; they'd stretch their neck fully forward, and open their eyes very wide; as if they were wondering... what will these crazy observers do next? It was silly fun, but no real satisfaction, not like with *Squilly*.

Rosemarie stayed hopeful. Maybe, *Squilly* would show up to surprise them one day. He'd jump from the roof, onto her husband's shoulder, playing in that same old way. It never happened... *Squilly* had a family now. If he was around, he and his family were totally camouflaged. They blended absolutely unrevealed, secretly masked by the other neighborhood squirrels. It took some time; but eventually Rosemarie accepted, it was better this way.

BEWILDERED
BY FAITH

The economy turned out to be a roller coaster ride. Their main concern became paying the mortgage. Month to month, they prayed for sufficient work, hoping to cover the expenses. They even began contemplating the need to move. The thought of leaving their home was overwhelming. This house had survived the American Revolution, the Civil War, and much more. How could they ever exchange heritage for money? It was a betrayal of self. They asked for wisdom, godly sense, to find the answers.

All these concerns made a good night's rest too difficult, so waking early became a habit. Rosemarie would make her way to the kitchen; fill the pot with enough water to brew the coffee; then think about *Squilly*. The heaviness of the uncertainties made her miss the little guy's visits; they'd brighten even a bad day. That dreariness would disappear, and she'd feel upbeat again—even happy. Rosemarie decided to prepare the coffee mugs—sugar and cream for Raymond, just cream in her own. She was thankful for this daily routine; it was a kind of cure.

Her husband was still asleep. Fortunately, careful attention to finances didn't make him nervous. The worried mind that accompanies concern, over providing for family needs, never keeps him awake. His faith and trust are strong. He believes the outcomes are already decided, distinguishing without a doubt that *"All things work together for good, for those who love God and are called according to His purposes"* (Romans 8:28); *"I will lie down in peace and sleep, for You alone, O Lord, will keep me safe"* (Ps 4:8).

Even with that, deeply as Rosemarie tried; her faith always seemed, to fall short. Her mind should've been set believing in the Glorious Risen Christ; in all His Power and Might. Instead, when she was most anxious she dwelled on the Crucified Christ; seeing Him on the Cross. Carrying an accumulation of guilt and blame and expecting the worst; she'd think to herself... *God allowed His Son to die! Why? How could He possibly grant my requests? In every respect I'm imperfect, a sinner; Christ was perfect, He died.* Her thinking was baffled.

In this believing capacity, there was only one conclusion she could see: *Oh well, whatever God wills—He'll do what's best.* Normally, that would be fine. Only, the negative outlook was depressing; so it created a disheartened attitude within her. Of course, she still pursued her intents. But, by entertaining this defeated state of mind; it was less likely her desired outcomes would ever be real. The view blinded her to the Truth. Christ *died* to save the world—He'll answer any worthy request. Every good desire *satisfies* His love for God's people! Rosemarie needed better understanding.

She lingered as the Mr. Coffee finished brewing, eyes gazing out the kitchen window. Remembering details about installing that window, all the awfulness came to mind. The Ciampis just purchased the house. Winter weather was on the way, and many windows needed replacing. Up to this point, the residence felt warm enough—comfortable even. Only, now temperatures were falling lower. Breezy currents of air, blew through the rooms from drafty, panes of glass. These upleasant conditions made the place much cooler.

Raymond wanted the job completed before the threat of snow; determining any sign of a storm might slow the progress. He'd gone outside to the garage. It was there…Wood moldings were being prepared. So the power saw was making fine cuts in the decorative trim. Without notice, the blade of the power saw caught Raymond's finger. Everything happened staggeringly fast. Rosemarie recalled only one thing—a feeling of total shock.

Commanding herself not to break down; she regained some sense of composure. Her husband needed immediate help, and she was compelled to oblige. Nerveracking thoughts began screaming " s*earch for any part of a finger!*" Quickly, Rosemarie scrutinized the floor in hope…perhaps the blade made a clean cut. That wasn't to be—there was only sawdust. It was clear any flesh disintegrated beneath the blade. Blood was everywhere. Honestly, the whole reality of the incident is still unbelievable, to this day.

There was even added challenges: fighting pain, struggling with emotional stress. These were unbearable for both of them! How was Raymond so incredibly calm? An actual peace and tranquility surrounded him. It seemed by relaxing, he was experiencing no strain or tension. This manner of Spirit is remarkably worthy of notice. In spite of the quiet self-control; her husband needed urgent treatment—attentive, medical care. Rosemarie rushed him to the emergency room.

Treatment took most of the day. But, with the pain medicine finally working; Raymond began to settle down. The couple could try to recover from the shock. However out of necessity; the pair was forced to concentrate on the missing window. The Ciampis needed a way to get the window installed. It was already dark outside; so they'd cover the opening with plywood tonight. Only Raymond was expected to be out of action, for at least three months.

The purchase of the home had stretched expenses to the limit. Nevertheless, they couldn't leave a hole in the kitchen wall for that much time; especially since it was winter. Raymond encouraged Rosemarie while instructing her with the plywood, "Rosemarie, you'll be able to install the window. I'll explain what needs to be done. I'm right here with you."

She certainly helped with enough window installations over the years; but install this herself? True, it wasn't a large window... She just wasn't sure it was possible. Rosemarie put aside the memories. She was just thankful Raymond's accurate direction and supervision guided the window's proper installation. Those feelings were a different story—about a noble restoration on their circa 1730 Saltbox Colonial.

Presently Rosemarie heard Raymond stirring. She reached for the coffee pot, and began filling two cups. Genuinely, both looked forward to the warm, early morning liquid. They appreciated the rich caramel color, and savored its fragrant aroma. Each would sip to enjoy the strong creamy taste that makes the first cup especially agreeable. However this morning seemed *unusually* quiet.

Every sign of activity around the primrose bushes was still. There was no goings on through the trees. Even the birds stopped chatting. And the squirrels typically dashing about... Where were they? Squilly's absence appeared all the more obvious. The odd silence seemed to have Raymond brooding. Remarking on the circumstance, he stated "It might become necessary to sell the house. Just in case, the home should be absolutely pristine." Then *grumpily* he stood up, and decided on a trip to the hardware store.

REAL AMERICAN SPIRIT

Rightfully, the Ciampis took pride in their American heritage. The couples' special home; representative of The United States, and The Thirteen Original Colonies; made a high-quality standard of workmanship important to the pair. Raymond always wanted to build, as far back as he could remember. Even at six or seven years of age, he'd already claimed his father's hammer as his own. His childhood was spent fascinated with imaginations, dreaming about the wonderful things he'd construct.

His young spirit of mind, envisioning new handiwork, pounded hard at objects and beat on wooden boards. It was no wonder the Ciampis chose this particular home—actually ending in possession and ownership of the remarkable house. Not just anyone would've rightly carried out the restoration, attentive to that foremost early American colonial character. Rosemarie and Raymond considered it their honor, a privilege to be of assistance in this way.

The two were giving new strength and meaning to the past through these efforts. They were taking part in the healing of history; making things better by renewing high standards, their forefathers achieved. This type of improvement would build up the home; using principle beliefs from an earlier time. The Ciampis' job was blending the methods—bringing together a valued way of working from the past, with the finest most excellent level, of quality from today.

Then, their home was guaranteed to be an accepted, highly respected restoration; yielding an established result—the already priceless worth and value; would be enhanced and strengthened to an even greater extent. Moldings, floors, paneling, even fireplaces; all were more than two centuries old! Stressed markings on the wood reflected generations of Americans; rightfully living here, in a different day.

Gentle slashes in doorframes were left behind as evidence; they substantiated distinct stages of growing children from past times. Hearths revealed menacing dark gashes that had been imposed by intensely heated steel pokers; the burning-hot tools used repeatedly over the years, to reposition the many burning logs. Even impeccably, well-maintained small areas of patched wood, earned recognition. Were these filled patched holes; perhaps buckshot damage from days of colonists, and Indians?

Maybe, shots fired during a war; one of great and

significant importance, told the true story of these outer doors. Rosemarie found a small musket ball during the restoration; it was beneath a threshold of the main entrance. Her body shook so terribly; she immediately tossed the round metal ball, into the woods. Envisioning a blood bath at the front door, removed any thought of historic significance, until later. But it was too late; the relic was lost to the woods.

These numerous untold signs, explained the workings of an incredibly, vital, essential past. Visibly, only a home of great consequence could've endured. This was all proof, the history of the United States was dealt a hard hand; and the fulfillment of the nation demanded a tremendous amount, from its countrymen. Nevertheless a heroic, noble American testimony; gladly accomplished, satisfying that order—reveling in joy—each Fourth of July, from past to forever.

Understandably sulking, about being forced to sell the home; Raymond set off to purchase some final supplies. Rosemarie began household chores—making the bed, and straightening the kitchen. Her thoughts were jumbled... *How can we ever sell this house? It's impossible! We've worked so hard here!* She glanced out the porch window, reminded of the last time they saw *Squilly* and his mate.

Addressing an invisible presence, and looking up, she asked "What could've happened to him anyway? Why the heck did he just disappear like that?" Obviously the guilt of leaving *Squilly* behind during their weekend getaway was long forgotten. Her mind, a whirlwind of questions, had no way to express the frustration. So childlishly, she stomped around the house saying "we just aren't moving!"

Her complaints were endless… *Why wasn't more work coming their way? And why was so much confusion in their life? At the very least, why couldn't Squilly show up, and visit so they'd feel better?* Even that confronted them—wondering over his disappearance. Couldn't anything be easy? All these demands were pointless; but the self-centered thoughts rambled on anyway. They invaded Rosemarie's mind making her more upset every minute.

THE CIAMPIS'
REVELATION

Then, at the most unexpected moment she was jolted, by this huge revelation—they really *might need* to move from their home. Self-absorbed, worrying over *Squilly's* disappearance, she never realized ... If he was around, they'd be leaving him behind, to face huge problems. New homeowners might not appreciate visits from a squirrel family. Seeing the animals as destructive, maybe they'd even use poison, to eliminate them.

That would be worse than the collar strangling him. Already trusting of humans, the squirrels would be targets. Their whole existence could be wiped out! The Ciampis would carry that guilt forever. Every trace of good accomplished by removing that collar would be undone. Their only memory of the squirrelly pair would be death and destruction—all joy would be erased. But God...! His infinite Wisdom orchestrated the whole situation.

The Spirit needed the Ciampis to understand that their will could've been accomplished. *Squilly* would still be coming around; and a *proud* flesh would love introducing the squirrel *they* saved. It would be *fun*. Except in the end, *Squilly* might lose his life. Then, Rosemarie and Raymond would hate each other for leaving behind a dependent, wild animal family—*Squilly's* helpless lineage.

Their wild friend brought his mate to meet the Ciampis for a purpose...The furry twosome was going away. Now starting a life together, the pair must leave to create a new generation of squirrels. Their natural instincts would provide, keeping the squirrel family independent and safe. The Ciampis could be satisfied with this result; they had trusted God. The Holy Spirit used Rosemarie and Raymond to achieve genuine good.

In this outcome, *Squilly* and his family are *really* saved; they live life relying on their Creator's care. If the Ciampis needed to leave for any reason; instead of mess and confusion; this was true, beautiful, unaffected life being left behind. God's Will accomplished! The faithful servant, rewarded for good work was given charge over all, his master's property. The Ciampis believed that servant must've had a similar emotion, because they felt worry-free! "*Job well done! Good and faithful servants*" (Matthew 24:45–47).

Yet like the faithful servant, Rosemarie wished charge over their property, would belong to them always. But finances were tight. There was a possibility the home would have to be sold. She knew the necessary strength, courage, and insight would be theirs; and they'd follow through with any, essential proceedings. Although, Rosemarie probably wouldn't understand, or be happy about the sale. The Ciampis *still* wanted their desires fulfilled. They were just selfish children in God's eyes.

The Holy Spirit needed the couple to understand... God's way is *always* best—His success is of a higher standard! Christian background identified with this truth, and some meanings were clearer; but everything seemed so challenging. She reflected about being faithless. It must be *extremely* demanding with only human nature to believe in. Thankful to trust in a Higher Power; Rosemarie was glad, she and Raymond, were used by the Holy Spirit. The experience had been a purposeful one.

She knew insecurity could've stopped them from doing His Will, and a wonderful opportunity would've been missed. The Holy Spirt had proved that trusting God works everything for good. Allowing Him control made their work effective—valuable to God's Kingdom. The Spirit revealed a very different ending, with man's nature in control. It wasn't a pretty picture. Her mind wandered... *things would be very different without our genuine belief and trust in God.*

First, the whole incident would probably be ignored anyway; yet having a good heart, the couple could choose to get involved. Only without proper confidence; fear and anxiety would play a scary role in stressful moments. They'd be happy about saving the squirrel, if lucky enough to remove the collar; but leaving for that vacation might be very different. Already having cared about the squirrel, once the couple realized the animal's welfare was endangered; they'd feel guilty for leaving.

The quarreling would take a whole other direction. Their loss of respect for one another; probably would result in some form of hatred, toward each other. Seeing a disastrous consequence in their future is easy. The inevitability of divorce becomes plain—their life together coming to a complete and total end. The probability of unbelief entering their existence would be strong.

That skepticism, to a greater extent, becomes directed toward God; causing fear that even a Heavenly Father won't keep His Word, in their destiny. Generally feelings of intense hostility can be produced by the split up. Those negative emotions end up triggering a disturbing amount of distress to family, friends, even business relationships. Everyone's cheated of their desired, anticipated outcomes—preferred conclusions and settlements, that are duly owed them.

Each person affected by the breakup, could acquire an irritated tendency; influencing them to expect the worst, from their surroundings. They'd be just waiting, taking for granted everybody around would deceive them, making themselves direct channels—transmitters of anger and resentment. All that bitterness has an adverse affect on the entire environment. These conditions are selfish and wrong; nevertheless there seemed to be no solution. Rosemarie's conclusion: *There could be no answer, without a genuine belief and trust in God.*

Thankful for her faith; she tried to tackle the extent of meaning, in this *alternative* outcome. She was never more grateful to know God. This was a crucial stream of understanding; and the couple needed to be familiar with this thinking. Listening to an assertive, deceptive reasoning from their flesh would be unjustifiable. The Holy Spirit had defined a clear moral code. Suddenly, there was awareness; it was a true gift that God's control over situations changes everything, for good.

Rosemarie understood—they *had* to hear God's voice. Only then, could the Spirit continue using them. Secure standards from Christian education supported this flow of inspiration. This fresh moral sensitivity made her cherish the value in Christ's message even more. It stirred up a faith and commitment to God in a whole new way. She anticipated her husband's arrival; and wished he'd hurry, back from the store.

A truly awesome God gave them a high position of employment in His service. His control eliminated fear and insecurity, making it possible to complete His Will. True to His promised Word; His security and peace lifted them from a painful ending of strife and confusion, to His perfect pride and peace. *"A peace that surpasses all human understanding"* (Philippians 4:7).

A TRUE MESSAGE

This new revelation was centered. Christ understood saving all mankind depended on eliminating selfish desires. His Father, creating the planet, fashioned man in His own image. Father and Son *know* the world; everything in it is beautiful, and worth saving. Rosemarie reflected on these wonderful beliefs. This was a true stream pouring out feelings.

Christ was born to live; because of *Him,* the world was saved. He *wanted* to live. The night before dying; He *agonized* asking if His life could conclude, any other way. Only the world can't survive with selfishness as the dominating force. Christ understood this so well, He ended by saying *"Not my will Father, but your will be done"* (Luke 22:42).

These disclosures were of such great magnitude that Jesus *allowed* Himself to die. Humanity *had* to understand…The only way to save the world for eternity was to put away selfish desire. Man gives life to himself by relieving others of burdens. Then, *that* rightful life passes back to the provider; and whatever measure one gives returns to the person. Someone generously giving receives what they gave and more; but selfish persons may lose even what they think they have.

"Take care what you hear, the measure you measure will be measured to you, and still more given to you. To one who has more will be given, to one who has not, even what he has will be taken away" (Mark 4:24–25).

The Spirit was unveiled in a remarkable way. Christ could've fought the soldiers when they came to arrest Him. He could've disappeared far from there, never speaking in public again. He'd already spoken the message to His own Jewish people. Many of Christ's people denied Him; they stopped listening. These people were jealous—knowing Him as a child they thought His greatness was impossible.

However, Christ knew human nature was jealous and petty. He never held this against any of them; the Love was extremely important to Him. Christ understood this new message of salvation would bring division; setting father against son, and mother against daughter. *"One's enemies will be of his own household"* (Matthew 11:34–36). This seemed confusing. The Fifth Commandment plainly says *"Honor your father and mother to have a long life"* (Exodus 20:12). *"Cursing father or mother will snuff out your life"* (Proverbs 20:20).

Obviously, it's easier to forgive an enemy a person never sees, than to forgive an enemy of one's house. Continually reminded of the offense by the deceitful relative's presence; the wronged person would find it difficult to let go of the resentment. Yet, a young child has no choice; they'll love an abusive parent anyway—because that's the young one's only lifeline. *"Turn from your sins and become as little children, or you will never get into the Kingdom of Heaven"* (Matthew 18:3).

The message became crystal clear. Loving an enemy is *really* possible, and absolutely crucial. It's not always under a person's control to make a situation right; but every person *must* do their best to keep peace. God *avenges* His enemies. Therefore, everyone should have an opportunity to be saved from God's terrifying wrath. *"God is a jealous and avenging Lord. He brings vengeance on His adversaries and wrath on His enemies"* (Nahum 1:2–3).

These truths would transform the whole world. So of course Christ wanted everyone to recognize; He loved His Jewish heritage and respected His Jewish religion, and culture. All this was plainly explained to everyone. Jesus had come to fulfill the law, every commandment—it was important to keep them. He and His disciples continued to honor and keep the Sabbath. Truth was brought to His own people first. This was key to the communication of His message.

This made it easily, visible to everyone that the teachings weren't just about some system, relating his human personal beliefs and values—a growing boy's learned traditions. The message was never about a system of religion, not then or now. If it was only about religion, Christ would've stopped telling the story. That would've been proof that the Jewish system of beliefs was His all important and only concern. But this true message was how to save the world!

These possibilities never occurred to Rosemarie.

The Spirit led her to respect this judgment: If man didn't give up his own desires to build up others, selfishness would destroy everything—all the world God created. Christ *knew* it was necessary to give up His own life, rather than allow that to happen. These calculations were *enormously* correct. He needed the world to see ... *Someone* was actually willing to die, because of the weight of these *Truths*.

Christ *knew* this was the *only* way God's creation could live life in "all its fullness." He died because it was the sole method; the one way, everything created by His Father would be saved. This was a true demonstration of His divine will. God's love for mankind was of such great consequence; Jesus approvingly wanted every good thing His Father fashioned, to be available—things like: beautiful mansions, rich foods, fine merchandise, jewelry.

Remarkably; His obedience in dying brought these things within every man's reach. Yet only those *honestly* following and walking in Jesus' way; may blamelessly and rightfully claim these promises. For that reason, every individual must humbly surrender to His loving kingship. Although regrettably, corrupt persons who scornfully mock Jesus' generous obedience, will be judged by His legitimacy.

"In my Father's house there are many dwelling places." (John 14: 2) *"For the Kingdom of God is among you."* (Luke 17: 21) *"'To love God with all your heart, understanding, and strength, and to love your neighbor as yourself is worth more than all sacrifices.' And Jesus said, 'You are not far from the Kingdom of God.'"* (Mark 12 : 33, 34)

Christ understood things can never keep man satisfied. Only love fully meets that condition. He *endured* the way to true life is dying to one's desire; each person giving of themselves to satisfy need, in others. Exclusively *God* imparts this wisdom. Rosemarie was raised believing Christ died to save the world. Though she never followed the *real* meaning in the words. Christ gave Himself to serve others. He wanted everyone to follow Him—saving the world with love!

He didn't want anyone to die anymore than He wanted to die. What Christ required was that every person would offer themselves, in service to help others. He wanted all people to understand the *Truth:* The value and worth of His life was great in God's sight; *uniquely* because He *freely* died to save the *entire* world—dying for God's creation to live!

Trust God's love for Christ and *feel* this meaning… God *respected* what Jesus accomplished. His Son gave up His *own* life for the worthy purpose of saving His Father's world—*complete* with everything and everyone in it. None ever need to die to save the world; Christ already did that. *Believe* in what Jesus accomplished. God could *never* deny His Son's wishes.

"God loved the world and gave His Son, whoever believes in Him will have eternal life. God did not send his Son to condemn the world but to save it. There is no judgment awaiting those who trust the Son of God" (John 3:16–18).

The only thing mankind *must* do is serve others by promoting a Spirit of Love—Love never dies! Only in this way, the world and everything in it will live forever. Rosemarie was in total disbelief. She'd never seen this light before. Right in front of her this whole time; terrorists were blowing themselves up, because they didn't understand this measure of weight—the matchless significance God places on His Son's death.

Having true understanding anyone can see, offering their body in death is an insult. God didn't want His Son Christ to die! Jesus was the first one to understand … Each must offer to serve others; that's the *only* way to stop selfish greed from destroying the world. God loved the world and everything it that much; He *allowed* His Son Jesus Christ to make a choice to actually die.

AN OPPORTUNITY
TO LIVE

Father and Son *know* man needed to figure the enormity of worth God places on His created universe. The whole earth had to be given the chance to understand... the door is provided. Only this *one way,* will save the world for future generations—*believe* Christ's accomplishment, open that door, save the world with love. Live an abundant life by serving one another. Learn and understand truth in Christ's message. There isn't anybody that should offer themselves in death for some greedy, excessive, seeking cause.

Rosemarie was never more thankful about the church for all they do to spread Christ's Word. The instant someone relates to the message; it's imperative to agree with this ideal on *how* to save humanity. Anyone identifying *real* truth regards creation of ultimate worth; paid with the immeasurable *irreplaceable* price of Jesus' decisive death. Everything is priceless, redeemable *solely* by a quality of life given up—the contentment in His life.

Once a person comprehends this correct Legitimacy; no person would tie bombs to *anything*—not themselves, or even anyone else. Saving the entire planet would be the greatest relevant affair. A great deal of meaning was in these special Scriptures; this unique gospel of John 15. Christ taught about himself, as being the true green branch; the beginning of new understanding! His life was being persecuted, because he came here to save the world.

"I am the true vine, a branch cannot produce if severed from the vine, remain in me to produce and any request will be granted… only they persecuted me, naturally they will persecute you, but I will send you the Advocate of truth, He will tell you about me, and you must tell others about me" (John 15).

Jesus explained greed and selfishness were completely evil. Innocent men would be allowed to die if they got in the way of greed's self-indulgence—even for working at something honest. Efforts as pure as spreading His message of truth could be life threatening. Still, He wanted all to be aware it was *necessary* for the message to spread. Man *had* to learn the importance of loving and serving one another.

Picture the death and destruction if love was never shared. With the branch becoming dry, and a message of salvation never told; the greed would consume everything. Eventually it could destroy the whole world. But the Holy Spirit always understood the world's needs, as completely then as today. The Spirit's very timely; He conveyed insight Rosemarie could never dream up, in a million years.

Essentially, Christ told us He was green. That is to say, Christ is the very first environmentalist. He died to save the world ... *to save the planet!* She became unbelievably aware of these words: *The Living Bible.* God's Word *is* alive. It's every bit as valid and applicable today, as when first written. If everyone understood His true message, people would build the planet's resources in alternative to tearing them down.

Instead of committing terrorist acts such as: bombings and polluting the water; men would invent new ways to save the world's wealth. Through this essential conservation, they'd protect and lift the entire environment, along with themselves. Rosemarie hoped to share this, she wished Raymond was here ... *why did it take so long to return from the store?* But it was just her impatient eagerness; there were so many different, thought patterns forming conclusions.

Her mind became engaged with issues about luxury. She genuinely agreed humanity was never expected to deny themselves. God created a wonderful world, making man in His own image. He anticipated everyone's happiness in these things—this was the same great joy He experienced on finishing His creation. The only thing He demanded in return was each person's love ... for Him, and for one another.

God's commandments to the world, really, are summed up in Love. *"Love God with all your heart, all your soul, all your mind. And love your neighbor as you love yourself"* (Matthew 22:37–40). He even explained what makes someone a neighbor. In that way, there could be no confusion. *"A neighbor cares for you. Shows mercy. Go and do likewise"* (Luke 10:29–37).

God never wanted anyone denied belongings. He wanted everyone living a full, beautiful life. But to live that life, any selfish wanting *must* be eliminated. Persons had to offer themselves to God above *everything* else. Next, they must generously help one another. Then, *all* His wonderful gifts are *abundantly* made available. This concept is so justly right it's almost beyond belief. Still, Rosemarie knew it made perfect sense. Her spirit was bursting with the new revelation. She barely held back the zeal, as Raymond walked in the door.

He began to display purchases on the counter. Rosemarie prepared him for a unique revelation, only discovered because oddly, a little squirrel showed up with a problem. Their every fear had been given to God. They dared to trust Him. Each agreed to His using them. By making a deliberate choice; both gave the Holy Spirit complete control of their actions. This was the commitment He required. That's how they were of service. The little squirrel was saved because of their obedience to the Spirit's direction.

His guidance saved *Squilly's* life, and ended the squirrel's suffering. Plainly, the Holy Spirit supported rescuing His little animal from harm. In reward, He made known all these original and fundamental principles. Rosemarie was convinced the Spirit hoped to use them again. Now, she had to assemble the discovery into a short, clear outline. It was important to be brief—there was so much information. Her prayer was apparent…The Spirit's conversation about saving the world *must* be stated properly.

SAVING THE WORLD FROM GREED

S he shared every conclusion with Raymond. Rightly the Message was obvious to both. Christ understood selfishness as an addiction that can never be satisfied—the more it's fed, the hungrier it gets. It powers itself by taking everything it wants; and never caring about the needs of others. Whatever stands in the way gets destroyed. Only one formula keeps those egotistical requirements satisfied...That need for self-indulgence must stay on top at all times. Selfishness and greed must push everyone beneath to continue in superiority.

Purposefully, carefully, Rosemarie considered the information. Would the Spirit give her wisdom to explain this correctly? Destruction and death could overtake everything; if selfishness attained that final element of highest degree. Facing an unpleasant end, this jealousy would make deliberate decisions *never* to be defeated. It would destroy anything in the way; ignoring all cost from its strength of will—what the outcome might bring about.

More than likely, this selfish greed would even consume itself, rather than lose higher rank or control. Now then, Rosemarie felt the need to inform everyone—these harmful attitudes could *unknowingly* determine the end of the world. The Ciampis were unbelievably startled. Both came to the same *crucial* realization. *Christ...* He'd *really seen* humanity must be saved; and openly died for the cause.

All these years they learned the teaching. Yet, even standing and living on those words, it never connected this way. Neither ever recognized the association. Their eyes just weren't opened. But now, each was *painfully* conscious of Christ's contribution. In letting Himself die, Christ gave man a bright path for life. Replacing all selfishness was Jesus' Perfect Love—turning, changing, converting man's arrogant mess and destruction.

His Father permitted the Son's death ... *only* to save His universe. However the Father knew His Son would live again. And in that resurrection, the Son's reward for saving His Father's world is the Father's entire Kingdom. His Son's accomplishment isn't required again—man's salvation is absolute. When Abel was murdered, his blood cried out to the Creator for justice. A righteous God would never allow sin to go unpunished, and Cain *had* to pay for his crime. "*Your brother's blood cries out to me, you are banished*" (Genesis 4:10–11).

Therefore it stands to reason; God honors and *sanc-*

tifies Christ's innocent blood *freely* shed to save the world. Every person loving God, and carrying out His plan *will* be raised with Him forever! Today's society is here, and lives *only* because centuries ago; Christ unveiled *unselfish* love was the one way to save the universe, from destruction. *"The sun will be darkened, the powers of heaven will be shaken… The Son of Man will come with great glory sending out his angels to gather his chosen from the farthest ends of earth and heaven."* (Matthew 24: 29, 31)

Even now, the creation of His universe *pleases* God so much; the world is given the Holy Spirit's peace. This comfort: If the world ever ends; all God's people will live together in a new paradise. *"Then I saw a new heaven and earth, the former heaven and earth had passed away, a voice called from the throne saying, 'God will always be with His people the human race, He will wipe every tear from their eyes,'"* (Revelation 21:1–4).

UNDERSTANDING SALVATION

Jesus Christ's ingenious generosity was almost too incredible. More than ever, it became clear that this new understanding was a pure river of life. Love for one another and respect for God's amazingly beautiful universe was the sole way to deliver the world. Christ figured out this vital world and everything in it must be saved. Creation came from His Father; so when this true message was denied Christ kept presenting the Word, to all mankind.

Due to their divine bond; Christ sympathized with His Father about the salvation of the world. Man had to be taught *real* love and Christ died for this cause. All peoples need to share this message of love with every generation. Value Christ's death—perceive the explicit picture. Love God above all. Love others with the same regard, as one's self. *Love…!* And it's only His selfless category, or kind of love that continues saving the world, even now.

Exceptional rewards belong to those people called to teach Christ's Word. These brave individuals give new generations the opportunity to follow a perfect plan for saving mankind. Educating people about Christ takes extraordinary courage. In the world, man selfishly wants—believing only his "small" way of thinking. Not interested to recognize a greater picture, he fulfills his prideful desire to be right, by doing exactly what's easiest.

So then, it's inconceivable that brave followers of Christ risk martyrdom, to share Jesus' true story. Terrorists, who never learn this real Love want to destroy these skilled instructors. Although; by blocking this flawless plan of world peace, and prohibiting nations from knowing these principal meanings; the universe would be doomed to destroy itself. The Ciampis were completely taken back… They'd never seen things in this light!

It didn't matter about religious beliefs. What mattered was that everyone, everywhere, knew about this amazing man Jesus Christ. He possessed all secret information about the insatiability of selfishness and greed. All humanity must conclude that self-indulgent powers left unchecked will destroy the planet, as it exists today. This perfect man uncovered the crucial problem; and gave His life for every eye to see and *unite,* in a selfless love.

Hearts were to triumph in Love's Salvation… With each person receiving respect, honor, and pride; having a proper admiration *only* in Christ's achievement—His life's ministry and Resurrection. Christ's cause wasn't self-importance and vanity. His death on a cross was an exclusive means of bringing light to the world. This was His only way of proving that love must have total control, for God's magnificent universe to survive.

A UNIQUE WAY

The Ciampis were overcome by the genuineness of Christ's ultimate gift. His selfless death provided all mankind an opportunity to choose eternal life. This *incomparable* path grants believers everywhere a method to share salvation, from generation to generation—family, friends, everyone can be saved forever! The reality had them speechless. Someone gave their life for others to live a full life. It was incredible ... This was the complete opposite of human nature.

There would never be enough lifetimes to thank someone for this kind of gained existence—the gift of content life. His death on a Cross removed all sin, sickness, and poverty. Then, the Victory over that agony brought about goodness, health, and prosperity. The world's only job is to believe His accomplishment and follow His pathway to life. The couple shared a decision: Their spirit committed to carry out God's Will always. They remembered a vital passage, "*If He begins a new work in you, He will not fail to complete it…*" (Philippians 1:6).

Both wanted Him to complete that work—not only in them, but in the whole world for that matter! They thanked Him for the revelation, and the peace He placed in their heart. The couple reflected their life, and talked about experiences, since being called to God's service. Giving the Holy Spirit control, they encountered many distinctive situations. If even some offer the hope that *Squilly's* story relates, just imagine the insight the Spirit is waiting to share.

The couple thought of God's greatness working everything for good. They wondered… *were more Ciampi life stories meant to be told? Squilly's* tale, recounted various times, had many marveling at the details—Rosemarie and Raymond still experience the sentiment. Their connection to the squirrel made his disappearance upsetting at the time. Yet, both admit their spirit improved through precious principles, acquired only by his going away.

Squilly learned through the Ciampis' disappearance. In the same way, Rosemarie and Raymond were educated when *Squilly* vanished—they discovered about real freedom. Encouraging their values, the Spirit trained the couple by helping both to surrender any covetous nature. Then directing about trust, He provided His strength and power, to believe God would provide for material needs. His instruction was clear… The pompous or self-important places one's invited to *or not invited to* aren't significant.

Similarly a wonderful home, enough food to eat,

and beautiful clothes is important; but real freedom comes from being independent. The couple achieved quite a breakthrough concerning this true self-sufficiency. It came from their *special* ties to a little squirrel named *Squilly!* They found independence can never be attained by shifting blame. This false sense of pride that causes guilt and doubt, only makes others afraid to speak their testimony.

The anxiety then, develops in an environment; spreading hate, deception, and damage everywhere. Truly independent people won't be controlled by anything but God—His love. Someone offering genuine love, gives the helped person a confident courage, to stand strong and operate in that love. Love is belief, trust, an unmistakable hope for the future; that the condition of one's existence will be of greater quality.

Love saturates everyone, everything, it comes in contact with. Soon the entire natural world improves in health, being lifted to a higher standard. The couple in complete empathy with the Holy Spirit understood it vital; every person had to be instructed in these laws of love. Sacrificing things will never make a better world. Only a giving spirit that's willing to serve others makes the entire world improved.

Everyone needed this Message … Love one another enough, be committed to family, build society. Acting in this way, every culture is raised higher, making all nations great. Then all individuals will finally survive this greedy civilization, that aims to keep all peoples in submission beneath itself. This type of self-reliance is real liberty, a true independence!

THE WAY OF LOVE

The Spirit's Words were sunshine.... The Message was bright, pure Light. Every person *genuinely* following Christ's way of love, saves the entire world. Being in His service, all needs and wants are provided by Him. Christ gave Himself freely. Every person must *willingly* offer him or herself, freely. That's each person's true cross. Instead of keeping a selfish lifestyle, be alive in this world for God. He'll *never* disappoint His people.

Christ proved the validity of these truths... He rose from the dead, and revealed Himself to those He loved. Man's spirit lives on for all eterity. Therefore, be sure to take part in *this* world's salvation. All must keep strict watch over their heart by guarding their words. Speak only what's good. Perform every action in love. Be involved in the solution. Then live on in the salvation—justly receiving any loving rewards contributed, and more besides.

The Scriptures gave luminous direction during this adventure with *Squilly*. Meaning and understanding was revealed, that can't be obtained any other way. These Passages lighten life's burdens. Each person should have the opportunity to read a *Living Bible*. This modern version is easy to understand. However, all Bibles contain many different books that offer strength, for overcoming life's situations.

Psalms is a book of prayers for *every* circumstance. And Psalm 91 is an incredible shield of protection ... In times of fear, a person can rely completely on the words. *Proverbs* is an organized guidebook for life. The instructive guide provides wisdom and perception for any situation. *The Gospel of John* explicity describes Jesus Christ ... As well as His incredible way, of saving the world. These are only a few of the books. Start with them to get familiar with the Spirit's insight. His caring nature really speaks to each individual on a personal basis.

Allow the instruction to light a way, and new observations will be revealed. Things a person sees their whole life become different, as if their eyes are finally open. It catches one unaware; yet the individual is thankful. Lines are drawn that begin to direct life's paths; opening doors that were never noticed, or even seen before. Most importantly, a person surprises themselves by acting in curiously new, and unusual ways.

Suddenly life's clearer, and a transformation takes place. At first, it's not really noticeable. Then, gradually in unexpected ways, one realizes their life isn't the same anymore. The funny thing is, it makes a person happy.

Certain in one's heart that selfishness is gone; problems resulting from greed lose control. The Holy Spirit influences the very inner core of someone's being—affecting them to restrain, and discipline their actions. This makes it clear the person's on the rightful road to life.

Therefore, when facing every decision... *Feel* His urging, trust His influence, and fear only God; *"He's the sole one who has power to throw body and soul into hell."* (Matthew 10:28). Belief and trust in Him awards a promise, *"He will keep us from the evil one."* (2 Thessalonians 3:3) Imagine it—*safe* from evil on the earth! Ask the Holy Spirit. He'll open one's heart and mind; satisfying each person with fresh insights into life. He has given His assurance, *"God shows no partiality. Whoever fears Him and acts uprightly is acceptable to Him"* (Acts 10:34–35).

He was even impartial toward His little squirrel. Just look at the care provided as the story unfolded. Can anything be less important than a wild squirrel? Nonetheless, the animal was saved... More importantly, the episode brought meaning and direction in the Ciampis' life. God's Power supplies unique understanding in *any* situation. Yet each person's heart will receive His information differently. For this reason, the Holy Spirit *completely* had His way in the writing of this book.

Christ cared enough to die so every person could live. Trust Him. Let go of every fear. Give any concerns to Him. Accept the truth of His salvation. Then permit Him charge, over every area of your life. His accomplishment is amazing. One's heart becomes filled with His life-saving, world saving peace! Truly, there will *never* be a greater peace than Christ's noble life being sacrificed, for all mankind.

If any person feels an urging to dedicate (or even to re-dedicate) their life to Christ—His way of saving the world—confirm the decision now! Tell Christ you love Him. Let Him know of your promise. Be sorry for *everything* wrong in you, or your life. Accept with no doubt that *"God loves the world so much, He gave His Son, everyone who believes in Him will not perish... they have eternal life."* (John 3:16).

"Praise Him" (Psalm 150). *"Thank Him"* (Psalm 26:7). Let Him know you're grateful for His magnificent wisdom—His perfect plan of saving the world. Allow *The Gospel of John* to fill you... Gain clear perception, and Christ's perfect knowledge. Consent to the Holy Spirit's guidance. He'll lead you to a church, where you'll be comfortable.

Tell your priest or pastor of the decision you've made. Then follow Christ's way of saving the world— love God above all; and love your neighbor, as you love yourself. Receive the support of the church. Let other Christian believers be aware of your commitment. In that way, you'll equip one another with necessary, courage to complete His Will. He'll walk with you forever, if you make room for him in your life.

Finally, walking in His perfect guidance; *"let your beautiful feet share His love, insight, and perfect life-saving peace anywhere His Holy Spirit urges!"* (Isaiah 52:7; Romans 10:15). Always remain confident—the gift of His perfect glorious Resurrection belongs to you and yours. And rightly, with God's fingerprint approving you for His service... Have a good and remarkable life!

A WORD FROM THE AUTHOR

Bible passages in the story are presented as a guide. They offer new direction and light. Many of the Scriptures represented are paraphrased. These particular passages are spiritual insight given to the Ciampis during various circumstances. Throughout their marriage, the couple gained inspiration using many translations of the Bible: *The Joyce Meyer Everyday Life Amplified Bible, The Catholic Study Bible, The King James Bible.*

Passages from these versions were all paraphrased in this story. Rosemarie speaks well of *The Living Bible*, urging that conditions in their life were exposed, and answers revealed by reading that particular version. Since the writing of this story, it has become increasingly difficult to find *The Living Bible*. The publisher, Tyndale Press, has been notified. They assure the version is in print.

The most recent publication of *The Living Bible* is called *The New Living Translation,* also printed by Tyndale Press. Many translations are equally enlightening: *The New American Catholic Study Bible, The New King James Bible, The Amplified Bible, The New International Version Bible.* These are only a few. There are *Patriot Bibles, Children's Bibles, St. Joseph's Bibles.* Any of these offer tremendous guidance, no matter what your age or preference.

Whatever version or translation the Holy Spirit places in your hands, be prepared—Truth will be revealed in your circumstances, light will shine on your life, and your spirit will be filled with new meaning. Allow God to raise you and never look back!

The author, coincidentally shares the same date of birth, with the well-known Reverend Dr. Billy Graham. Many years ago, the wise Reverend shared these words, *"Let the Holy Spirit teach each person what He wants them to understand."* The author, in complete agreement with his words, prays the same for everyone reading this book.